For my two daughters, Fern and Sofia,
with all my love - R.W.

For lovely little James - G.P.-R.

First edition for the United States, its territories and dependencies, and Canada
published in 2004 by Barron's Educational Series, Inc.

First published in 2003 by Orchard Books, 96 Leonard Street, London EC2A 4XD,
United Kingdom.

Text © copyright 2003 by Richard Waring.
Illustrations © copyright 2003 by Guy Parker-Rees.

All inquiries should be addressed to:
Barron's Educational Series, Inc.
250 Wireless Boulevard
Hauppauge, NY 11788
www.barronseduc.com

International Standard Book No.: 0-7641-5801-5

Library of Congress Catalog Card No.: 2004102088

Printed in Singapore
9 8 7 6 5 4 3 2 1

Ducky Dives In!

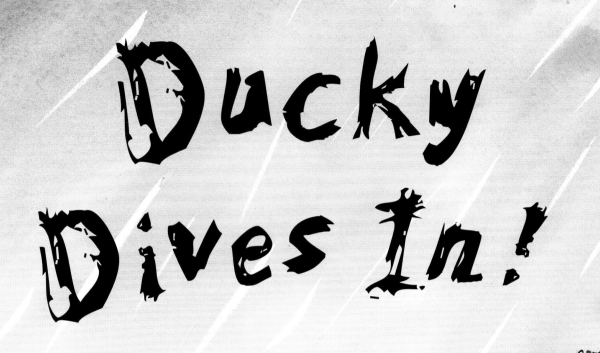

Richard Waring

Illustrated by Guy Parker-Rees

There was once a duck who loved to be mucky.
He loved puddles and anything…

slimy,

squishy,

and slushy.

The more he could splash,
the more he would quack...

and then quackle!

And cluckle...

and chuckle!

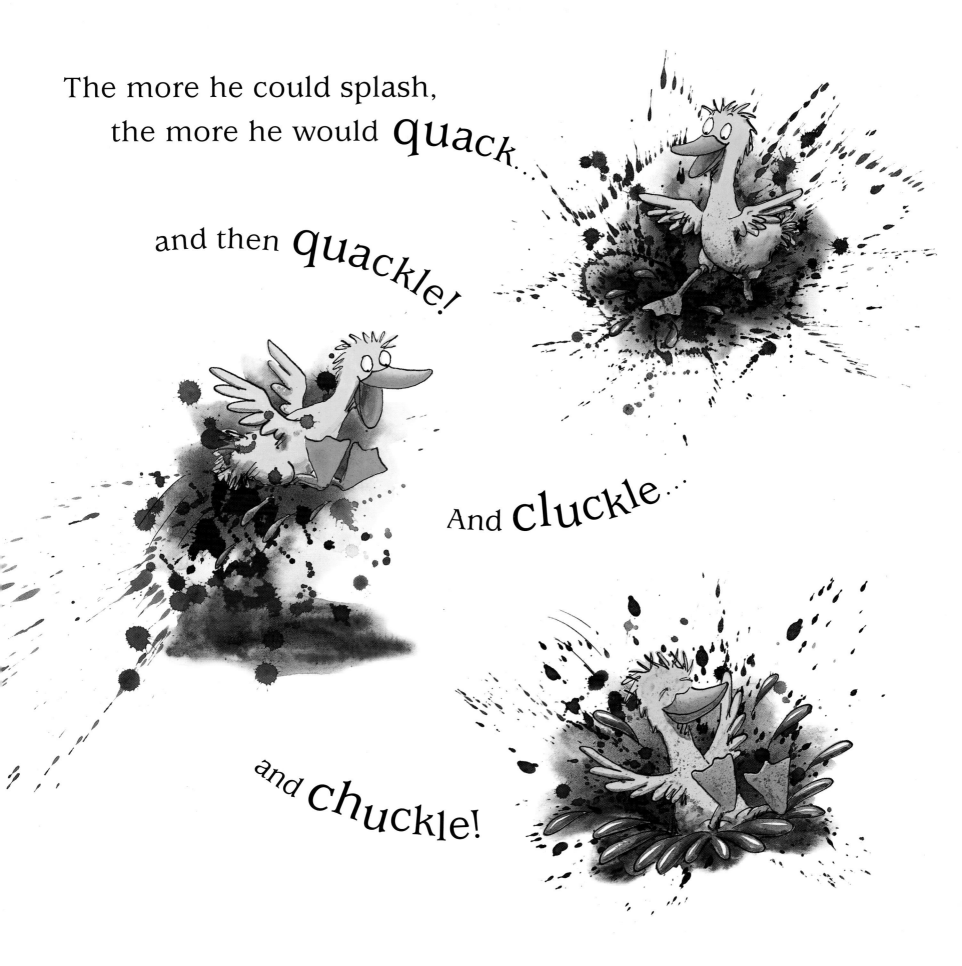

But whenever Mucky Ducky
sneaked off to splash in
the sloppy old pig trough,
he would suddenly hear
a very loud…

QUACK!

And there would
stand Mommy Duck – and
Mommy Duck would march
him back to the big pond.

She would scrub him until he shone.
And as she scrubbed she would sing,

"A scrub-a-dub duck! For a good little duck
needs to be squeaky-clean!"

So whenever Mucky Ducky
was about to jump into
the slimy stream,

or the dirty puddle
in the pigpen,

or hide under
the leaking gutters
by the sheep shed...

he would hear a

QUACK!

And there
would stand
Mommy Duck.

Mommy Duck wanted him to shine
and sparkle and be neat and clean.

Now, behind the woodshed,
down a little path,
was an old millpond.

Most of the time the millpond was dry and
the mud at the bottom was hard, so no fun at all.

But when it rained, the hard mud turned squishy
and soft and slippery and sloppy.

And one day it rained…

and rained...

and rained.

And Mucky Ducky
plotted and planned.

And waited…

While Mommy Duck was looking the other way, Mucky Ducky crept silently up the side of the bank.

Mommy Duck did not see him.

He sneaked through the bushes,

and ran past the flower beds.

And still Mommy Duck did not see him.

But as he crawled through the clover patch, the tip
of his shiny yellow tail wiggled just above the grass.
And Mommy Duck saw it…

and she wondered…

and she looked up at the rain…

then down at the pond…

and then she remembered the millpond…

and
Mucky
Ducky!

And off Mommy Duck dashed.

She took a shortcut right through the slimy stream,

She hurried under the leaking gutters by the sheep shed,

then ran through the dirty puddle in the pigpen.

and even over the squishy swamp,
        until finally Mommy Duck saw Mucky Ducky.

But Mucky Ducky had
almost reached the edge
of the millpond! Mommy Duck
ran as fast as possible toward the pond.

Mucky Ducky got nearer and nearer
to the mud as Mommy Duck
ran faster and faster and
got closer and closer.

And just as Mommy Duck
was about to reach out
and grab Mucky Ducky...

she slipped on her slimy,

muddy foot and started to slide and slither

along the path...

and splashed into
the middle of the
grubbiest,
dirtiest,
squishiest

pile of mud in the whole farm!

Mucky Ducky looked at Mommy Duck.
Mommy Duck looked at Mucky Ducky.

Mommy Duck said quack...

and then quackle!

And cluckle...

and chuckle!

squished and **slushed** together,
all day long.